THE KISSING BOOTH ROAD TRIP!

This book belongs to

....

This World Book Day 2020 book
is a gift from your local bookseller and
Penguin Books

#ShareAStory

CELEBRATE STORIES. LOVE READING.

This book has been specially created and published to celebrate **World Book Day. World Book Day** is a charity funded by publishers and booksellers in the UK and Ireland. Our mission is to offer every child and young person the opportunity to read and love books by giving you the chance to have a book of your own. To find out more, and for loads of fun activities and reading recommendations to help you to keep reading, visit **worldbookday.com**

World Book Day in the UK and Ireland is also made possible by generous sponsorship from National Book Tokens and support from authors and illustrators.

World Book Day works in partnership with a number of charities, who are all working to encourage a love of reading for pleasure.

The National Literacy Trust is an independent charity that encourages children and young people to enjoy reading. Just 10 minutes of reading every day can make a big difference to how well you do at school and to how successful you could be in life. **literacytrust.org.uk**

The Reading Agency inspires people of all ages and backgrounds to read for pleasure and empowerment. They run the Summer Reading Challenge in partnership with libraries; they also support reading groups in schools and libraries all year round. Find out more and join your local library. **summerreadingchallenge.org.uk**

BookTrust is the UK's largest children's reading charity. Each year they reach 3.4 million children across the UK with books, resources and support to help develop a love of reading. **booktrust.org.uk**

World Book Day also facilitates fundraising for:

Book Aid International, an international book donation and library development charity. Every year, they provide one million books to libraries and schools in communities where children would otherwise have little or no opportunity to read. **bookaid.org**

Read for Good, who motivate children in schools to read for fun through its sponsored read, which thousands of schools run on World Book Day and throughout the year. The money raised provides new books and resident storytellers in all the children's hospitals in the UK. **readforgood.org**

THE KISSING BOOTH
ROAD TRIP!

BETH REEKLES

PENGUIN BOOKS

PENGUIN BOOKS

UK | USA | Canada | Ireland | Australia
India | New Zealand | South Africa

Penguin Books is part of the Penguin Random House group of companies whose addresses can be found at global.penguinrandomhouse.com.

www.penguin.co.uk
www.puffin.co.uk
www.ladybird.co.uk

First published 2020

001

Set in 11/18 pt Palatino
Typeset by Jouve (UK), Milton Keynes
Printed and bound in Great Britain by Clays Ltd, Elcograf S.p.A.

A CIP catalogue record for this book is available from the British Library

ISBN: 978–0–241–43856–5

All correspondence to:
Penguin Books
Penguin Random House Children's
80 Strand, London WC2R 0RL

Chapter 1

'You haven't booked the tickets yet, have you?'

I winced, hastily turning down the volume on my computer as Lee Flynn, frantic and frowning, popped up on FaceTime. I looked from him to the Google Chrome window on my computer screen. Two seats to JFK, baggage included, one for Mr Lee Flynn, one for Miss Rochelle Evans.

'Dude, you don't have to yell. I'm literally doing it *right now*. I'm just picking our seats. You're getting the aisle seat. I know you said you like the window, but you'll be getting up to pee, like, all the time, and I just can't deal. You know it's costing about twenty dollars extra *each* to add –'

'Abort mission, Shelly,' my best friend since forever shouted at me. Lee leaned closer to his phone until I could just see the top half of his face, his forehead creased and his eyebrows knitted together. His dark brown hair was stuck up at odd angles and his blue eyes pierced right through the screen. 'Do *not* book the flights.'

'What? But . . .'

My mind rattled. Why didn't he want me to book the flights? We'd been planning this trip for weeks. Spring break was coming up and we'd decided to mark the occasion with a trip across the country. It was our senior year of high school, we had been working our butts off to get good grades for college, and we deserved the break.

Plus, Noah, my boyfriend and Lee's older brother, was currently in his first year of college in Boston on the other side of the country, which I had to admit was a big factor in me wanting to visit the East Coast. I wasn't entirely selfish, though: Lee's girlfriend of about a year, Rachel, had just been accepted to Brown, which was only an hour's drive from Harvard. Rachel and her parents were going out to take a look around the campus. While I spent time with Noah, Lee would head down to Rhode Island to meet up with Rachel.

The plan had been to fly into JFK in New York and to drive to Boston from there, but not before spending a day in New York to visit a few of the tourist traps. I was so excited to see the Statue of Liberty. I'd never been to New York before. Actually, I hadn't really left California much before.

We had it *all* planned: an epic trip to celebrate our senior year.

And suddenly Lee was yelling at me to 'abort mission'?

'Did you and Noah have a fight?' I demanded, scowling at him. Lee and his brother had an unshakable bond – but they didn't always see eye to eye. I should know. I'd watched them grow up together, and I knew both of them well. Lee and I were the same age (to the day) and we'd been best friends our entire lives. Our moms had been good friends, too, until my mom passed away in a car accident when I was younger.

Lee and Noah never had *big* fights, though. The only time I'd really seen them fight properly was last summer, when Lee found out that Noah and I had been secretly dating. (I still felt guilty about not telling Lee, even though he'd forgiven me. It was the only time I'd ever lied to him.)

'No, we didn't.' Lee hesitated.

'Did you and *Rachel* have a fight? Lee, what the hell is –'

'I screwed up,' he blurted, holding his phone further away so I could see his whole face. I was hit with the full force of his puppy-dog expression – which didn't *always* work on me. 'You know how I was gonna sort out the car rental?'

'Yeah?'

'So, it turns out nobody will rent to us because we're not eighteen.'

I groaned and leaned over my desk, pressing my hands to my face. The news shouldn't have surprised me. I was usually the more organized of the two of us (something I attributed to having looked after my little brother, Brad, a lot). Lee could be much more spur-of-the-moment. Of *course* he hadn't noticed the age restriction until the very last second.

Exasperated, I cried, 'Lee! You said you checked it all out!'

'Well, yeah, I thought I did! You know, I googled and it said there were extra fees if you're under twenty-five sometimes, but that's fine. But . . . then I thought maybe I could rent it in Noah's name –'

'Lee!'

'But my mom overheard me asking him about it on the phone –'

'Oh my God,' I huffed. I loved my best friend more than anything, but sometimes he could get a little *too* carried away. 'Please tell me you weren't actually planning on doing that. I'm pretty sure it's, like, a crime.'

'Spare me the lecture. My mom already yelled at me over it. I told her I was joking, but . . . it's not like Noah was even going to go along with it, as it turns out. I mean, seriously. He was the resident bad boy at school, always getting into fights and skipping class. He used to *smoke*. A few months at Harvard and suddenly he's Mr Goody Two-Shoes?'

I rolled my eyes. Annoyed as I was that Lee had *actually* been considering that as our next-best option, I couldn't help breaking into a smile as he talked about Noah like that. Despite being our high school's resident bad boy, as Lee had put it, Noah had changed a lot since going to college. Everyone else used to find him totally intimidating, but Lee and I had known him better. I'd harbored a helpless crush on Noah since I was, like, twelve. It turned out to be not-so-helpless when we ended up dating last year, after making out at the charity kissing booth Lee and I had run at our school's Spring Carnival.

College might have tempered some of Noah's bad-boy attitude, but he was still our Noah.

Still my *Noah*, I thought, my stomach fizzing and warmth spreading through me.

As soon as it crossed my mind, the worry started to seep in. I hadn't seen Noah since Christmas break, and, well, he had changed a lot since going to college . . . I *hoped* he was still my Noah . . .

I shook the thought away quickly. Everything would be just as it always was between us. It had to be.

'Anyway,' Lee said suddenly, tearing me away from thinking about my boyfriend. He had a bright smile on his face that I hadn't been expecting. 'Don't book the flights. We'll just drive the whole way instead!'

'What?'

'Well, it was hardly a road trip, was it, Shelly?' he wheedled, raising his eyebrows at me. 'Just New York to Boston?'

'It was five hours, Lee.'

'*Exactly.* You couldn't get out of Texas in five hours.'

'Just how long *is* the drive from here to Boston?' I asked, opening a new tab to look it up. I hadn't even been driving for a year and I definitely hadn't done a long drive – let alone cross-country.

'Like two days,' Lee told me so quickly I almost missed it. 'And if we take turns driving and nap on the road, we'll be there in no time.

Plus, school's shut for an extra week, because they have to fix all those busted pipes, remember, and get all the electrics fixed and stuff? We'd have plenty of time to drive there and back, *and* still hang out once we get there.'

A sensible voice in the back of my head told me this was completely ridiculous. Even if we did take turns driving and napping, it'd probably take us a week to get there. It was a crazy suggestion. We should just fly to Boston because, duh, of course that was the easiest thing to do.

But Lee and I didn't do easy.

We did, however, do crazy.

My dad would probably sigh and rub his eyes and ask us if we'd really thought this through. Noah would laugh at us and tell us we'd barely make it out of California before giving up, turning round and jumping on a plane. Lee's parents would probably roll their eyes and throw their hands in the air, knowing they couldn't talk us out of it, and give us plenty of gas money, and Lee's mom would insist that we text at regular intervals so she'd know we were safe.

As I ran it through in my head, the nagging, sensible voice got quieter and quieter until it disappeared entirely and Lee's voice took over.

He hadn't noticed my wandering thoughts. He was too busy telling me he didn't even mind me driving his precious '65 Mustang convertible, how much more fun the whole thing would be than flying, and didn't I want to drive cross-country? And we'd be doing *the* bucket-list item, the thing everyone wanted to do some day. We'd be free of our parents and responsibilities, and it'd just be us and the open road. It would be, like, a rite of passage. And *totally* grown-up – going all the way across the country to spend some time with our other halves and to hang out at college, no less. We could still go to New York, Lee promised, even if it was just to drive through . . .

'Come on,' Lee pleaded. 'This is our *senior year,* Elle. This was supposed to be our year. Remember? Our grand finale to high school. This could be our last great adventure before the rest of our lives!'

He finally stopped to draw breath. His eyes glittered and his mouth split into a beaming smile as he waited expectantly for my decision.

'Lee,' I said gravely.

I heard him gulp, waiting to be shot down.

'Pick me up in ten. We've got road trip snacks to buy.'

Chapter 2

June Flynn hugged her son tight, then turned to hug me just as closely. 'Now, drive safe, okay? Stick within the speed limit. I swear to God, Lee, if you come back with a single speeding ticket, you'll be grounded until your college graduation. And you, miss . . .' She turned to me with one eyebrow arched and her arms crossed. 'You keep him in check, Elle, do you hear me? And neither of you drive if you're too tired.'

'We know, Mom.' Lee sighed.

I'd just had pretty much the same conversation – for the dozenth time – with my dad before I'd come over to Lee's. Brad, my eleven-year-old brother, had been sulking and complaining loudly for the last few days. Lee and I had only broken the news about our coast-to-coast road trip to our parents after we'd planned our route, decided where we wanted to stop and made a playlist. Brad was desperate to join us – he'd even given Lee the cold shoulder until we were leaving . . . which was a big deal. Brad *idolized* Lee.

'Can't I go with them, though?' he'd begged Dad.

Lee had crouched down and clapped a hand on Brad's shoulder. 'Hey, buddy,' he whispered loudly. 'Look, between you and me . . . it's gonna be *really* boring. We're gonna be stuck in a car for *days*. And there'll be traffic. If you really want to get stuck in a car with your sister for almost a week . . .'

Brad thought about it for a minute, pouting, before asking, 'Will you send me pictures if you stop somewhere cool? And get me a souvenir from New York?'

'Cross my heart,' Lee promised.

June's lecture was carrying on in the same way my dad's had – although she told Lee to listen to me and reminded me to look after Lee, whereas my dad had made Lee swear to watch out for me, and told me to listen to Lee.

'And if you do get in an accident –'

'I know the drill, Mom. Dad's told me what to do a hundred times. I've got insurance, and Noah taught me how to change a tire. We've got this.'

June pursed her lips for a long moment before throwing her arms round both of us. 'I'll be tracking you on Find My Friends.'

'You never should've taught her how to use that,' Lee muttered to me. I just shrugged. I wasn't overly sorry. I'd had more than a few texts from June asking if I'd heard from Noah, she hadn't heard from him in a while and was worried about him, she assumed I would have talked to him and, if I hadn't, that she was right to worry. Eventually, I'd had enough, and showed her how to use Find My Friends so she'd stop worrying so much.

We finished saying our goodbyes. Lee's old '65 Mustang convertible was already loaded up with our bags, plenty of snacks and drinks and some blankets. We'd put together a fifteen-hour, thirty-two-minute playlist for the trip, and Lee had replaced the stereo system in his car a while back, so we could plug in our phones.

June waited on the porch to see us off, her cardigan wrapped round her and one hand up to block the sun from her eyes. Lee checked his mirrors and started the engine as I buckled my seatbelt. He had the roof down so I pulled my hair into a ponytail to save it from the wind. I unhooked my sunglasses from the neck of my tank top and put them on, then plugged in my cell. Spotify was open in one app, our route in another.

My phone buzzed. It was a text from Noah. My heart skipped a beat and I cradled my phone as I read it.

Can't wait to see you in a few days. Got so much cool stuff planned for when you get here xxx

Lee's seatbelt clicked into place. The first song started up. It was Lee's choice: Rihanna's 'Shut Up and Drive'. He beamed at me, his blue eyes glittering in the sunlight, his dark brown hair pushed back from his face, and his fingers flexing round the steering wheel. He revved the engine, his eyebrows waggling.

'You ready, Shelly?'

'Ready,' I told him. My mind drifted to my reunion with Noah. 'Now, shut up and drive.'

When you think about it, driving almost nonstop across the country for four or five days doesn't *actually* sound like much fun. I mean, sitting in a car all that time, getting stuck in traffic, grabbing quick bites to eat at fast-food restaurants. Plus, we actually had somewhere to be, so we weren't stopping to look around every new town, or going to see the World's Largest Ball of Twine, or visiting the Shoelace Museum or whatever it was we passed.

Brad *definitely* would've hated it.

But four hours in, we'd almost made it to Arizona, and I was loving every second.

Ever since Lee and I had first talked about taking a mini road trip from New York to Boston, I had been picturing it in my head: a cute, mellow indie tune playing (probably featuring a banjo), Lee and I laughing, the windows down, and the sun shining on our faces. I'd told myself it was just a fantasy . . .

But that was almost exactly how it was right now.

Admittedly, the song playing wasn't by some banjo-backed indie band. It was a duet from *Les Mis*, and Lee knew every word. Rachel was in the drama club and *Les Mis* was this year's school production, and Lee, always the dutiful boyfriend, had practiced with her a bunch. He'd added a ton of show tunes to our playlist, actually.

'Come on, Shelly,' he cried out, his face creased with laughter. 'You promised you'd sing the other parts!'

'Why can't I be what's-her-name? Why do I have to be Eddie Redmayne?'

'Because I'm *always* Marius. I never get to be Cosette. Just give me this, Shelly. Let's start again. Hand me another Red Vine?'

I passed him one. We'd rationed the snacks carefully before leaving, and I was on snack ration duty while Lee was behind the wheel. I was glad we'd thought ahead – otherwise we'd have easily blown through two days' worth of snacks by now.

It was the fifth time Lee had played this song, so I was starting to remember most of the lyrics. Lee was actually pretty good, but he sang with a terrible exaggerated French accent. I kept bursting into giggles, no matter how hard I tried to keep a straight face. We'd had to turn up the stereo really loud to hear it over the wind and the noise of other cars, but when Lee couldn't keep it together any more and broke off halfway through a line, all I could hear was his laughter.

The roof was down and the wind whipped around us, tangling my hair and blowing Lee's into a total mess. The sun was a little hot, but I didn't mind at all, and the sky was the kind of bright blue that's never as nice in a photo, no matter how much you play with the filter. The road stretched out ahead. Palm trees had been replaced by scrubland, and brown-grey mountains lined patches of the horizon.

The sun and wind were in my face, Lee was hooting with laughter beside me, and there was the promise of the trip still to come. I'd never felt so free.

Chapter 3

We stopped for burgers for dinner, then I took over the driving. Lee had eaten so much at the diner that he fell asleep after maybe ten minutes, so I switched our playlist to a podcast instead. We'd sung so much during the first part of the drive that my throat was actually kind of sore. (It was so worth it, but I needed to rest my voice before the next epic singalong.)

The roof of the car was back up, and I put my window down a little. The night air was cold and refreshing. Without the lights of the city, the sky was inky black and scattered with stars winking silver and white.

Sometime around midnight, my phone rang. I pressed the Bluetooth button on the stereo and answered the call.

'Hello?'

'I can't believe you guys are driving all the way from California to Boston,' said a deep, smooth voice that made my heart skip a beat. My face melted into a smile.

'Noah. Hi.'

'You know, if you guys had just got on a plane to Boston and given up on the road trip, you'd be here already.' Noah gave a soft sigh. It was even later for him. I guessed maybe he'd been at a party or something. I pictured him lying on his bed, one arm propped behind his head as he stretched out, a slow, slanted smile on his face that showed off the dimple in his left cheek. I imagined his eyes half-closed, how easily I could slot in beside him and kiss his neck.

I kind of wished I was there already.

'You're on speaker,' I told him.

'Hi, Lee.'

'He's asleep right now,' I said after a beat. 'But, you know. He might wake up. Or, knowing him, he'll be pretending to be asleep so he can eavesdrop and use this conversation to tease me for the next few days while I've got no escape. So don't say anything that'll embarrass me too much or be too soppy.'

Noah laughed. 'How's it going so far?'

'Pretty great! We've even got leftover snacks from today. Honestly, I thought we'd eat through the entire trip's worth before we even got out of the state. And we've only almost crashed once.'

'What?'

I waved a hand dismissively, frowning with irritation as I remembered. 'Some guy swerved across our lane to take an exit off the interstate at the last second. There were a *lot* of cars honking. We didn't tell your mom that part when we called her from the diner.'

'Probably for the best.'

'How come you're up, anyway? It's, what, two in the morning for you?'

'There was some late-night bowling thing. I tried to bail before the karaoke started.'

I sat up straighter, grinning. '*Please* tell me you did karaoke. There had better be videos.' I could *not* imagine my badass motorcycle-riding boyfriend doing karaoke. 'Tell me you got roped into singing something totally corny, like, like, I don't know, "Blue Suede Shoes".'

There was a home video from when we were kids of Noah and Lee's mom singing along to 'Blue Suede Shoes' on the radio. Noah was in it too, at maybe eight or nine years old, dancing along and imitating all of Elvis' classic moves and singing half the words wrong. His parents had found the video a couple of weeks ago and Lee had saved it to his phone in case he ever needed to blackmail Noah.

'What's wrong with "Blue Suede Shoes"?'

'Are you telling me you sang "Blue Suede Shoes"?' I teased, grinning.

'I definitely did not do karaoke,' he told me gravely. 'But I did definitely get videos of the other guys doing it. Great blackmail material.'

Noah and Lee were scarily alike sometimes, for all their differences.

'So, are the other guys . . . um . . .' My fingers drummed on the steering wheel. I gulped. 'Are they doing anything for spring break?'

'A bunch of people went down to Florida.' I could practically *hear* his eye roll that went along with that statement. He perked up a little when he added, 'Including Steve.'

Well, that was welcome news. Up until a couple of days ago, Noah's room-mate still hadn't decided how to spend spring break. I was relieved we'd have the room to ourselves.

'A few people went home, but a lot are still around. Some of the football guys, a few people from my class . . .' Noah cleared his throat. 'And, uh, Amanda's sticking around, too.'

I digested that news for a moment. I could understand why he sounded so awkward and stiff: Amanda was part of the reason we'd broken up for a while last year. A picture of Amanda kissing Noah's cheek at a party, her arms wrapped round him, showed up online. I found out Noah was hiding a secret from me that she was in on, and I became convinced he was cheating on me. I'd broken up with him, breaking my own heart in the process.

And then he brought her home for Thanksgiving.

Obviously, we worked things out. Noah wasn't cheating, but he had been hiding that he was struggling with a lot of his college classes from me. He and Amanda were just friends.

Sometimes I still had to work on being cool about it and not overreacting. They were close. Amanda was an affectionate person. But, I'd remind myself, Lee and I were close too, and there was definitely nothing romantic between us. I had to trust Noah when he said that his friendship with Amanda was similar. He gave me space to let that sink in, too, which I appreciated.

I'd seen Amanda a couple of times when I'd been on FaceTime to Noah. We followed each other on Instagram. And she was so darn nice that it was impossible to hate her even if I'd wanted to. (I'll admit, sometimes I did want to. I was jealous that Amanda got to spend so much time with Noah, and that she had a connection with him I'd never have.)

I guessed this was how Rachel felt about me and Lee, though. I swallowed my pride and jealousy, and said, 'That's great! We'll have to all grab dinner together. It'll be nice to see her again.'

Noah didn't do a good job of hiding how relieved he was by my reaction. His sigh whistled down the phone, and he said quietly, 'Thanks, Elle. She's really excited to see you again too, you know.'

'She didn't feel like going home for the holidays?'

Amanda was British and her parents lived somewhere in England, which was why Noah had invited her to the Flynns' house to celebrate Thanksgiving. (Although, at the time, I didn't know that. I'd believed they were in a relationship.)

'She's signed up for some volunteering project throughout spring break. You know, to boost her résumé for when she starts applying for internships. Besides, her folks are off on some cruise round Europe. She said she didn't fancy being stuck on a ship with them for two weeks straight.' He laughed at some joke I clearly didn't get.

'Ha-ha. Right. Well, hey, if there's another bowling-and-karaoke night, we should go. I bet me and Amanda can drag you up on stage.'

'You wish,' he chuckled. 'Ugh, I can't wait to see you. Can't you just pull in at the nearest airport and take a flight?'

'It's only a couple more days. We're making great time, you know. We're already in New Mexico. Besides, do you really want me to give up the spring break of a lifetime, driving cross-country with my bestie, just so I can spend more time making out with you?'

He didn't even hesitate. 'Absolutely.'

I laughed. 'Shut up.'

'I'm serious. You know what, when you do get here, forget about seeing Boston. Uber Eats exists. We don't even have to leave the room. We'll spend the whole time together.'

I flushed, then shot a quick look at Lee. His head was tipped back and he was drooling with his mouth wide open.

'I guess I'd better let you go,' Noah said, yawning and mumbling his words. 'Don't wanna distract you too much.'

I rolled my eyes, grinning. 'Oh, please. Just admit you're sleepy.'

'Could stay up all night talking to you, babe.'

'You want me to take you up on that?'

'Goodnight, Elle,' he said. 'I love you. Get here soon, okay? Drive safe.'

'Love you, too. Now get some sleep, you big goofball.'

Noah hung up and the stereo switched back to my podcast. I felt the ache in my chest I got when I really missed him. It felt like forever since I'd last seen him, even if we talked every day. Knowing I was only a couple of days (and a few thousand miles) away from seeing him somehow made the ache worse than ever. Being apart so much was so difficult. And, after spring break, I wasn't sure when we'd next see each other.

I squared my shoulders and adjusted my hands on the steering wheel. No. It was no good thinking like that. I didn't want to waste any of the next few days moping over how much I'd miss him afterward.

Right now, I was on the road trip of a lifetime with my best friend. I wasn't going to let what-ifs about Noah get me down. I was going to make this the best spring break ever.

Chapter 4

We traveled through the cities that lined the I-44 in Oklahoma, watching the landscape turn greener, thicker and lusher. By the time we made it to Missouri, Lee was getting cabin fever.

So far, we'd only made one stop that wasn't for food or gas: Miami, Oklahoma.

As we'd entered the town, Lee told me, 'Come on, Shelly, we've gotta do something on this trip that's not just driving to Boston! This is the dream! This is the best time of our lives! And, hey, now we can tell everyone we went to Miami for spring break.'

'You know we've gotta *show* people, right?'

He caught my eye and grinned. We took a quick bathroom break at a diner to change into our swimsuits, then got someone to take a photo of us jumping in the air in front of a sign reading MIAMI. Lee even found an inflatable flamingo pool float at a convenience store (which was now sticking up from the back of the car, too big to fit in the trunk). We got plenty of weird looks from the locals, but the photo also got plenty of likes on Instagram from our friends, jealous at how much fun we were having on our road trip.

That brief stop-off had been a couple of hours ago, and it had only made Lee more determined to get off the road for a while and *do something*.

Lee tore his phone out of its holder on the dash and tossed it into my lap so he didn't have to follow Google Maps any more. He leaned forward with grim determination, his eyebrows furrowed together and his mouth pressed into a thin line.

'What the hell, Lee?'

He didn't respond.

'You want a snack?'

Still nothing.

'Here, have some –'

'I don't need a snack,' he snapped. 'I need to get out of this car. We're in Missouri, Elle! There must be things to see and do in Missouri! Come on, look something up.'

He turned to me now with bulging eyes and a twitching smile.

'You think you've maybe had *too much* sugar, Lee?' I asked, but I obligingly looked on the map to see what we were near. 'Eyes back on the road, buddy.'

He sighed, slumping down. 'Sorry, it's just . . . This is a *lot* of driving, you know? And we're not even halfway there yet.'

'We're basically halfway there. Give or take a couple hours.'

But I got his point. Our carefully curated playlist and a few podcasts had helped keep us entertained, but we were just . . . driving. There were only so many BuzzFeed articles and tweets we could read aloud, and while one of us drove, the other one usually napped anyway.

It turned out road trips weren't exactly glamorous.

Our little impromptu photoshoot in Oklahoma had given me a taste for spontaneity and adventure, too. Nobody was around to tell us what to do. We made our own rules. Noah could wait a few extra hours. What was a few more hours when we hadn't seen each other in months?

And besides, right now those few hours felt like the most exciting and important thing Lee and I could indulge in.

'Okay, got it!' I exclaimed after a few minutes of research on my phone. 'We're coming up on the Mark Twain National Forest . . .'

Lee groaned. Beaches were his thing. The woods? Not so much.

'Hey, you're the one who said you were sick of looking at roads, mister. We're gonna go see some trees and eat our lunch there.' I reprogrammed the destination on Google Maps and wrestled his phone back into the holder. 'It'll be cute. We'll have a picnic. Send your mom some photos. Maybe see a deer.'

'As *if* we're going to see a deer.' He thought about it. 'Ten bucks we see a bear.'

'Do they even have bears in Missouri?'

'Ten bucks.'

I shrugged and took the bet, thinking I'd much rather have my lunch interrupted by Bambi than a bear. I texted the family WhatsApp – which consisted of me, Lee, Noah and our parents – to let them know about our change of plans. My dad and June were both nervous about Lee and me driving across the country and they liked regular updates.

Lee turned up the music, now singing with gusto as he bounced his head and drummed his fingers along to the song. Having a new destination in mind that wasn't just the next gas station seemed to have cheered him up.

Honestly, I was kind of looking forward to the break, too. One more unscheduled stop wouldn't hurt, right? We had plenty of time.

We sat on top of a rock just off the start of a hiking trail in Mark Twain National Forest, hidden away from the rest of the world in a cute spot by a stream surrounded by trees. We dug into the sandwiches we'd bought at a place called Bixby's, which was recommended on both TripAdvisor and a YouTube channel I'd found. We got a pie there, too. Mostly because I couldn't resist the delicious aroma, but also because Lee argued that we'd had pie in every state so far, and now we had to find out which state had the best pie.

(He had been updating his Instagram with lengthy reviews of each state's pie. I kind of couldn't wait to see what he had to say about Missouri's, and whether or not it would beat out the weird-but-somehow-wonderful combo of mint and cherry we'd had in New Mexico.)

'See, this is the life.' Lee sighed, tearing off another mouthful of sandwich, then using the sandwich to gesture out in front of us. The sunlight filtered through the trees above us, casting him in a green glow. 'Isn't this the life, Shelly?'

'If you ask me that one more time, I'm throwing your sandwich in the stream.'

'Hey. Didn't you see the signs? No littering.'

'I'll keep the wrapper. Just toss the sandwich. A racoon'll eat it.'

'A racoon would never appreciate this bacon the way I do,' he told me gravely. He looked me in the eye as he took another slow, deliberate bite of the sandwich, then rolled his eyes back in his head as he moaned. I laughed so hard I choked on my own food and had to gulp down half a bottle of water to stop coughing.

We'd walked for an hour to find the spot where we were now sitting. We hadn't meant to go so far, and it surprised us both how much we'd needed to get out of the car and stretch our legs for a while.

Occasionally, we heard someone else on the trail passing by. For the most part, though, the only sounds we heard were birds, rustling leaves and the burble of the stream.

It was just us.

It was . . . pretty glorious. Even Lee was mesmerized.

Our quick pit stop rapidly turned into an afternoon off by the time we'd finished the sandwiches, eaten half the pie and drank a bottle of iced tea. It'd take another hour to walk back to the car, but neither of us had made a move. This was exactly the kind of adventure we had been picturing when we'd planned the road trip, I knew.

Lee and I stretched out on the rock. We were lying down with our heads near each other's knees.

My cell phone buzzed. I looked at it and saw it was a text from Noah – he hoped we were having a nice afternoon. Guilt fizzled in the pit of my stomach.

'We should get back on the road,' Lee said. He didn't even need to ask who the text was from. It had been maybe five or twenty or forty minutes since I'd said the same thing – it was hard to keep track of time while in a drowsy food-induced haze, basking in the afternoon sun and listening to the wildlife.

'You wanna take the night shift or shall I?'

Lee grumbled incoherently but I knew exactly what he meant. We shouldn't have stopped. It was getting increasingly impossible to think about going back to the car. Neither of us was thrilled at the idea of sitting behind the wheel and driving for eight or nine hours. Not when this forest was so idyllic.

Lee rolled on to his side, almost kneeing me in the face. I propped myself up on my elbows and raised my eyebrows at him, knowing some grand proposal was on the way.

'Okay. Just hear me out,' he said. 'What if we stuck around here tonight?'

My nose wrinkled before I could help it. 'What, camping? You hate the woods. Now you wanna camp out? We don't even have a tent.'

'No, I just mean . . . in Missouri. St. Louis isn't far. They've gotta have something going on tonight, right? We'll just . . . extend this little detour. And then, I swear, no more stops like this. Come on, Elle. How many times in your life are you gonna be in Missouri?'

I laughed. He said it with all the grandeur of Paris or Venice, or somewhere else romantic and starry-eyed.

But, hey, I guessed they didn't set *Meet Me in St. Louis* in St. Louis for nothing.

Lee's mouth drooped, his eyes widening into a puppy-dog look.

Oh, shoot. Who was I kidding? That look *totally* worked on me.

We'd already lost half a day – what was a few more hours?

Lee was right. How many times in our lives would we be in Missouri?

Between the two of us, Google and Facebook, we found an outdoor concert being held that night in a park in St. Louis. Local bands and musicians were playing. There were going to be fireworks.

I beamed at Lee, the guilt of delaying seeing Noah completely gone. The excitement of the night ahead consumed me. 'This is going to be so epic.'

Lee hopped off the rock. 'Come on. It's three hours to the city, and that's without traffic. You can buy the tickets on the way.'

We hastily collected our things, and it was only as we were leaving that I gasped, grabbing at Lee's arm and dragging him back. 'Look! Look! I told you!'

He whispered, 'Whoa.'

Right there, not even fifty yards away across the stream, was a deer.

It ran off when I took a photo. The flash was on – something I only realized once it was too late.

'You're an idiot.' Lee wrapped an arm round my shoulders and led me back up to the path as I pouted and cursed myself. 'Send that to my mom, huh?'

'Sure. And you owe me ten bucks.'

'Aw, come on. We're not out of here yet. Might still see a bear.'

I rolled my eyes and elbowed him in the stomach. He reached up to ruffle my hair and I ducked away from him, laughing.

I spent most of the drive to St. Louis asleep. The concert only went on till ten, when the fireworks display was due to start. We grabbed a blanket from the car and found a spot in the crowd. Lee got talking to a group of college-aged guys nearby who gave us some drinks, and I got us hot dogs from a stand. We shared some of our road trip snacks with the guys and they recommended a motel nearby where we could spend the night.

'You're a cute couple,' one of them told us.

'We're not –' I started. I was used to strangers assuming we were a couple, but Lee cut across me.

'Oh, yeah, she's a total sweetie pie. I've never known *anyone* fart that loud while sleeping in my life.'

The guys looked like they didn't know whether to laugh or look away. I draped my arms round Lee's shoulders and leaned over him to say, 'And you should see his daily skincare routine. Nobody rocks a sheet mask like this guy.'

One of them caught on and broke the stunned and slightly awkward silence with a burst of laughter as he realized his mistake.

The group left a little while later to go and meet their other friends who'd just arrived, leaving me and Lee behind. We watched the bands and ate cotton candy as we waited for the fireworks. Lee sighed and leaned his head on my shoulder.

'This is what spring break should be, Shelly. Us, the open road . . .'

'Random concerts in St. Louis?'

'Yup.' He sighed, and there was something nostalgic to it. 'I'm glad we did this trip, Elle. Next year . . .'

He never finished the sentence, too busy daydreaming, but he didn't have to. Next year . . . who knew what would happen? We still didn't know where we were going to college – maybe it wouldn't be the same place. I hoped it would be, but . . .

Maybe next year, Lee would want to go to Florida for spring break. Maybe I'd want to go home to see my dad and brother. Maybe I'd spend spring break traveling somewhere with Noah, and Lee would be the one who wanted to go home.

Neither of us knew what the next year would bring. But we did know that we had right now.

We held hands as the fireworks went off. I took some pictures to send to Rachel and Noah later on. I didn't know if Lee and I would be able to spend time together like this after the summer. For now, it was beautiful.

Chapter 5

We drove almost nonstop through Illinois (where there was barely a hill or a mountain in sight), past the cornfields of Indiana and along turquoise Lake Erie in Ohio (which we decided we definitely couldn't miss seeing) to make up for all the extra time we'd spent in Missouri. Each state seemed even greener than the last. It was a different world to what we were used to in California.

We drove *almost* nonstop . . . We did hang out for a while at Lake Erie, watching the sunrise and eating breakfast before I took over the next driving shift.

I could tell from Noah's texts that he was a little annoyed by our detour in Missouri. I confronted him about it over the phone at a gas station while Lee used the bathroom and bought more drinks, and Noah gave in.

'I'm sorry. I know you guys had a blast, and I'm glad you did. The deer picture was cute. Amanda loved it. I just – I *miss* you, Elle.'

I softened at how quiet and sad his voice had become. 'I miss you, too. But, you know, how many times are we gonna be in Missouri?'

'You get me a souvenir, at least?' he asked, and I knew all was forgiven.

We had, in fact, been buying plenty of souvenirs. We'd bought refrigerator magnets in every state – two in each so we both had one, of course. And we'd taken pictures at every state line, or as near to it as we could stop.

After I hung up, I went into the gas station and bought Noah the lamest thing I could find: a keychain that said 'O-hi-o there'.

We climbed back in the car and I checked the route on the map. The quickest route to Boston might have been to carry on along the lake and drive up past Buffalo, but we were trying to hit as many states as we could (without being too crazy) and we *really* wanted to visit New York City, just like we'd planned from the start. We were still planning to see a play on Broadway. So, instead of traveling further north, we added a couple of hours to our trip by heading back south toward Philadelphia. That way, we'd be going through Connecticut and New Jersey on the way to Boston, too, where we could add a couple of extra magnets to our collection.

I zoomed out a little too far on the map by accident, and something caught my eye.

'Hey! We're not that far from Detroit!'

Lee raised an eyebrow. 'What's in Detroit you wanna see?'

I shook my head, screenshotting the map and then going into my text messages. 'Nothing, I guess. It's just where Levi's from.'

Our buddy Levi had been new to school at the start of senior year after moving from Detroit, and he had easily fallen into place in our group. While Lee was focusing on football and Rachel, and while Noah was all the way across the country, I'd grown pretty close to Levi. Very close, I guess, since he'd had a crush on me, and I'd kind of made out with him at Thanksgiving. But that was water under the bridge, and he was one of my best friends. I mean, he was no Lee, but nobody ever would be.

I'd actually thought it would've been kind of nice to have Levi along for the road trip, but I hadn't even *considered* suggesting it. This trip was about me and Lee, and Boston was about me and Noah. Adding Levi to the equation would have been . . . messy.

I texted Levi after sending him the screenshot. *Check out where we are! Totally going to detour to your old place to stalk your old friends and find out embarrassing stories about you.*

Lee didn't say anything, he just nodded. I'd told him there was nothing between me and Levi and that I wasn't interested in him, but whatever I said Lee remained unconvinced.

He bit the inside of his cheek in silent judgment, which reminded me that I really had no right to get mad about Noah and Amanda's friendship. They, at least, had never kissed.

'Don't,' I told him.

'I didn't say anything.'

I rolled my eyes. 'Oh, please. Like you even had to.'

Lee shrugged, holding up his palms in surrender.

My phone buzzed with a reply. *Please, Lake Michigan is waaaay more interesting if you do head out that way.*

And then: *BTW, hung out with Brad earlier. He's missing Lee. Like, a lot. I'm teaching him lacrosse this afternoon. You guys so owe me.*

I showed Lee the message, and he laughed. 'He's such a pushover.'

'He's just nice. Brad really likes him.'

'Buuuut not as much as he likes me.'

'Hmm, you *have* abandoned him for spring break to drive cross-country with yours truly. I dunno. Last time you ditched an Evans for a girl, they got pretty close with Levi . . .'

Lee shoved me. 'Get driving, Evans, we've got places to be. And I did not ditch you for Rachel.'

'You so did.'

'All right. Maybe a little. But you know I love you.'

'I do. Did you get me a Diet Coke?'

Lee paused. 'Shoot.' And just as I'd put the car in gear to drive off, he unbuckled his seatbelt and leaped out the door to run back inside.

Lee took over driving just before we got to New Jersey. I fell asleep somewhere near Newark and, when I woke up, I was completely disoriented. It was late afternoon, and the Manhattan skyline was nowhere near as close as it should be.

But – it was totally breathtaking.

Fluffy grey springtime clouds gathered in the sky above the city, reminding me of a snow globe.

'What . . .' I rubbed my hands over my face, then sat up and combed my fingers through my hair in an effort to wake myself up. The clock on the dash showed I'd been asleep for almost two hours . . . during what was supposed to be a thirty-minute drive.

'What's going on?' I asked.

'Welcome to the Big Apple,' Lee said, sounding tetchy and jerking his arm around. 'The city that never sleeps. Or stops driving, apparently. I've barely moved for, like, forty minutes now. You know how I know that? I got through a whole podcast, and we're no closer to the city. I called my mom. She said there's been a really bad accident, and there's roadworks going on, too. This is worse than rush hour.'

'Oh, damn.'

Bumper to bumper and surrounded by honking horns, it wasn't the movie-worthy scene of the unforgettable spring break we'd been imagining. I couldn't help laughing at the look of pure exasperation on Lee's face, though.

'You should've woken me up,' I told him. 'We could've played I spy.'

'I spy . . . something beginning with "s"?'

'Hmm . . . Is it . . . skyscraper?'

'Bingo.' His chuckle quickly turned into a sigh as he shook his head. 'I called Noah, too. He said we should just turn round, avoid Manhattan altogether.'

'Well, I mean, I guess we could –'

Lee cut me a look. 'I did not sit in all this traffic to *not* get into the city, Elle. Besides, my mom's already looking at Broadway tickets for tonight. She's gonna call back when she's found a good deal for something she thinks we'd like.'

'I could've done that.'

'I didn't wanna wake you up,' he said.

I smiled. Lee could drive me crazy sometimes, but he was a sweetheart. And would he even be my best friend if he didn't drive me crazy?

Then he added, 'Not when you were drooling like that. I grabbed a *great* picture of you to send to Noah. Mouth wide open, nostrils flared, at least three chins going on . . .' He mimicked the pose, which was both hilarious and mortifying.

I self-consciously wiped one hand around my mouth and chin, then smacked Lee's arm.

Would he even be my best friend if he didn't embarrass me?

Before I could joke back at him, he was focused on switching lanes and the smile slipped from his face. So far on the drive we'd been loving it, but right now Lee looked more stressed than I'd seen him in a long while.

Gently, I said, 'Hey, we could always come back through on the drive home, you know.'

Lee shook his head and tightened his hands round the steering wheel. His knuckles turned white. 'No. No, we're doing this now. We're not *that* far away. And –' He cut himself off with a sudden sigh, and his shoulders slumped. 'I'm sorry. It's just . . . this is just how we planned it, you know? This trip is supposed to be perfect.'

I squeezed his hand nearest me. 'I know. I'll look up parking near Broadway, okay? We can plug it into the map, then.'

'Thanks, Shelly.'

I think we both knew, really, that it didn't matter. We could skip our little stop in New York and visit on the way home instead, or we could plan another trip for the summer. If the trip didn't go exactly to plan it wasn't the end of the world . . . Right?

But it *was*. Looking at Lee's face, it was absolutely the end of the world. This was our big plan and our epic spring break, and we'd loved the idea of going to New York on the way to Boston. If we didn't, it would spoil everything and we'd be leaving New York with a sour taste in our mouths. We wouldn't even be able to sing along to our playlist any more. Sure, being spontaneous was great. When things you can't control get in your way, well, you've just gotta deal and move on . . . But this wouldn't be like that, I thought, determination setting in. We'd be giving up and admitting defeat, and turning our backs on this adventure and all the grand ideas we'd had for it.

Neither of us were willing to do that. We were going to make this trip everything we'd imagined it to be, and nothing could stop us.

So we sat in traffic, inching along toward the city. When Lee's mom called to let us know she'd grabbed the last two tickets online to *Hamilton* for an absolute steal, I put the soundtrack on and broke out the emergency snacks to cheer up Lee.

He cheered up pretty quickly. Soon enough, he was talking about spending time with Rachel and her family at Brown and saying, 'I could fly into New York. Meet her here. We could see *everything*. All the plays. Has she ever told you about her pipe dream to move to New York one day? I mean, she calls it a pipe dream, but I think she could do it, you know?'

I had to smile, listening to the way Lee talked about his girlfriend. He was utterly head over heels for her.

'Speaking of seeing everything, I don't think we'll get to see the Statue of Liberty,' I told him. I tried not to sound too disappointed. I'd been *really* looking forward to seeing it. But then, we hadn't planned on arriving in New York so late. All that time in Missouri had really thrown off our plans.

'Shelly, if you can put up with me singing *Wicked* when I can't hit any of the high notes, I can get you to the Statue of Liberty. You just watch.'

An hour before we had to be at *Hamilton*, Lee was navigating the hellish roads of New York, cursing every other second and flinching whenever a cab swerved round him because he was driving too carefully. We found somewhere to pull in to watch the sun set over the Hudson and admire the Statue of Liberty.

After a nightmare afternoon, the day had turned into a total dream.

Chapter 6

I felt sick as we drove through the towns and forests in Massachusetts. We made great time through Connecticut and arrived near Boston, following the directions to Harvard University. I could hardly even think about how gorgeous the river looked when we drove past it, or that we were right by Fenway Park, or how quaint the red brick buildings were.

I checked my makeup in the mirror on the visor for the hundredth time. I'd insisted we put the roof back up on the car so that my hair wouldn't be a total mess when we arrived at Noah's dorm. My mascara had smudged. Had I rubbed my eye? Shoot, why wouldn't it come off? And now I'd messed up my concealer . . .

'Stop panicking,' Lee told me, laughing. 'You look great, Shelly.'

'I look like I've spent the last four days cleaning myself with baby wipes and using dry shampoo.'

'You got to shower at the motel in Missouri! And that gas station in Texas had showers.'

'We must stink.'

Lee shrugged. 'Like he's gonna care.'

'I care!'

I rooted around in my purse. I'd run through an entire pack of deodorant wipes in the last hour. The ramifications of our almost nonstop road trip were now *really* getting to me. I knew I had some perfume in there somewhere . . .

I finally found it and spritzed myself, half choking Lee. He said, 'Seriously. Stop worrying. You look just fine.'

'Just fine?' I echoed. My voice was shrill. I gulped, trying to bring the octave of my voice back down. 'I can't look "just fine", Lee. I haven't seen Noah in months. I'm supposed to look – I'm supposed to look *fantastic*. I'm supposed to look sexy and gorgeous and effortlessly pretty and –'

'And not have lipstick on your teeth?'

'Shoot.' I snapped the visor back down and bared my teeth in it before turning to glare at Lee. He couldn't hold back his laughter as I smacked his arm. 'That wasn't funny! Can't you see I'm having a crisis here?'

'Oh, you're having a crisis? What about me? Spare a thought for your poor old best bud, who's going to be bunking on some stranger's floor so you and my brother can have some quality time to yourselves.'

'Noah told you, you can have Steve's bed.'

'I really don't need to be across the room while you two are making out and spooning in bed.'

I rolled my eyes, but I didn't argue with him. Was it really so bad that I was kind of glad Lee had refused the offer so Noah and I could have some space? Alone? It made me feel like a terrible best friend, but I was so desperately excited to see Noah I couldn't *really* care.

Although, now I was less desperately excited and more just . . . plain desperate. I was stinky and bedraggled from all the travel. My hair was stiff – probably from using way too much dry shampoo. I'd eaten pretty much nothing but junk food for the last few days, so I felt as disgusting as I was sure I looked.

And I just knew that when I saw Noah, he'd look as hot as ever.

Nerves started to coil in my stomach as we got closer to campus, but not so much over the way I looked any more. What if Noah had changed? When he'd first come home after going to college he'd started growing a beard, he'd switched up his wardrobe to be more mature-looking, and he'd given up his stupid habit of smoking cigarettes so he smelled different, too.

What else would have changed since I last saw him?

I knew my fears were totally irrational. We video-chatted a lot. We sent pictures. I knew what he looked like.

But . . .

I couldn't let go of the nagging worry that there would be something unfamiliar about him, that this time it might be like meeting a stranger. Maybe, despite all the phone calls and texts, things wouldn't be the same between us as I remembered.

I had shredded a Kleenex into confetti by the time Lee finally drew the car to a stop.

We were here.

'Hey,' he murmured, reaching for my hands. I met his gaze and bit my lip as his warm blue eyes softened and his mouth pulled into a gentle, encouraging smile. 'Relax. Okay?'

I nodded, then followed Lee as he got out of the car. Noah had text us with instructions on how to get to his dorm, and I was only half aware of Lee tapping at his phone on the walk. He was probably telling our parents we'd arrived safely.

I looked around but still took nothing in. All I could focus on was how awful I probably looked, and my growing dread that Noah would open the door to his room and the chemistry between us would suddenly be nonexistent.

A brick building loomed over us that I recognized from photos Noah had sent me. I sucked in a breath and closed my eyes for a second, hooking my hands round Lee's arm.

'Well, well,' called a voice, 'look what the cat dragged in!'

My eyes snapped open.

And there he was.

Noah. My *boyfriend*. Tall and broad and swooshy-haired, wearing a red flannel shirt over a tight white T-shirt that showed off his toned torso and abs. He wore distressed jeans and his ridiculous big boots that I loved so much – that were so quintessentially Noah. He beamed at us and waved. He'd shaved his beard off completely. I could see the glint of his bright blue eyes, the dimple in his cheek.

And, just like that, I let go of Lee, dropped my bags (and my dignity right along with them) and ran at Noah.

He caught me and lifted me into the air as I flung myself at him. His lips met mine before either of us could say another word. I was glad

I'd spent the last hour popping Tic Tacs. Noah's arms curled tightly round me and he set my feet back on the ground, his lips still not leaving mine.

'You guys are disgusting!' Lee yelled. 'Shelly, I'm not carrying your bags for you.' I knew he would, though.

My fingers knotted in Noah's hair and we pulled apart to catch our breath.

'Hi,' I whispered.

'Hi,' he murmured back, and kissed me again. He only stopped when Lee, now standing beside us, cleared his throat. He dropped our bags to give Noah one of those brief one-armed guy-hugs with plenty of pats on the back.

'How was the drive?' Noah asked, collecting my duffel bag from the ground before I could protest.

'Which part?' Lee laughed. 'And, hey, what's the deal, you're not offering to carry my bag? I'm your little brother. How dare you pick some girl over me.'

'I'll carry your bag, Lee,' I told him.

'I thought you were a star football player now,' Noah shot back, smirking. 'All macho-macho. Carry your own bags!'

'I never used the words macho-macho.'

'Someone did.'

Lee glowered at me, pouting, but I held up my hands. 'Hey, wasn't me.'

'Oh, it definitely was,' Noah said.

I swatted his arm. 'You're supposed to be on my side.'

'Always, Shelly.' Noah winked at me, and I felt my heart somersault enough times to win gold at the Olympics. Lee had called me Shelly for as long as I could remember, although I hated it when other people did. But when Noah called me Shelly, there was always something teasing about it, something . . . Something that made my stomach fill with butterflies.

I hopped up on to my tiptoes long enough to peck him on the cheek and slipped my hand into his as the three of us walked toward the dorms. Noah told us that Amanda's room-mate had gone home for spring break at the last minute, so Amanda was going to bunk with a friend and let Lee have her room while he was here. Noah led us there first, and as we walked we made plans to meet for dinner that evening. Amanda, obviously, would be joining us.

Predictably, Amanda enveloped me in a huge hug when she saw me. With an excited squeal she said, 'Hi! Oh, it's so great to see you again! How was the trip? Noah showed me the pictures. It looked amazing. How was *Hamilton*? Lee! Get in here!' She let me go so she could hug Lee, too, while still asking us questions and barely taking a breath, let alone giving us space to answer her. Amanda was overwhelming, but in the best way possible. She was wearing yoga pants and a soft pink sweater with equally soft fuzzy pink slippers. Her blonde hair was pulled up in a high ponytail and she wasn't wearing makeup. She didn't need it. I could see her freckles. I swear she got cuter every time I saw her. And I'd forgotten how great her British accent was. She made it impossible to dislike her.

She took Lee's bags and summoned us inside, listening attentively as we talked about the show, the sunset and the Statue of Liberty, the funniest moments from the drive, and how great our impromptu stop in Missouri had been.

While we chatted, Noah flung himself on to a desk chair. He rocked back dangerously far and propped his feet up on the edge of the desk. Amanda walked over to push his feet off the desk and prop up the chair before he fell, her eyes and smile still on us as Lee hunted through his bag. I was glad Lee was talking; I would've faltered. The action looked so familiar, so normal for them – totally second nature – that it threw me. It was exactly the way Lee and I acted.

I looked around the room as Lee launched into the epic retelling of his pie-by-state comparisons (Pennsylvania was currently on top, but we had yet to have pie in Massachusetts). Amanda's dorm room was exactly like I'd pictured. It looked like something out of a catalogue. There was a sprawling leafy green plant on a shelf over the desk and a fern beside the bed. A thick grey knitted throw was draped artfully over the foot of the bed on a white comforter. It complemented the pink pillows. Even her laptop cover was pink. Her books were organized by color and there was a cream-and-gold tapestry on the wall. Her room-mate's side had more greens and blues, but it was equally pristine. *Her* books were organized alphabetically.

It was like Amanda had looked up 'cute dorm rooms' on Pinterest and pulled one of the rooms straight out of her phone.

I hated how much I loved it.

I was checking out a snow globe of Edinburgh when Amanda said, 'Have you ever been?'

'Huh?'

'To Scotland? Or, well, any of Britain?'

'No. I've, well, I've never been to Europe. Never been to the East Coast before, either.'

'Next spring break,' Lee told me, 'we're going to Europe.'

'If you do, you absolutely *have* to go to Barcelona. It's just divine. There's so much culture. And the art there . . . They have an entire

Dali museum. Have you ever seen any of his work?'

I stole a glance at Lee, who looked every bit as lost as me. Noah just shrugged. I'd seen on Instagram that Amanda followed a lot of art galleries and went to museums and stuff, but I didn't remember her talking like this over Thanksgiving. (Although, admittedly, I'd spent most of Thanksgiving thinking she'd stolen my boyfriend and trying to ignore her.)

Amanda noticed the awkward silence and said quickly, 'It's a gorgeous city. There's really something for everyone.'

'Speaking of something for everyone –' Lee dug through his bag, pulling out a big box of fancy chocolates. 'My mom got me this to give you. To say thanks for having me, you know.'

Amanda took the box, saying a sincere thank you, how thoughtful, how kind.

'We should kick these guys out one evening and have a girls' night,' she told me with a grin. 'And eat our way through this with a trashy movie.'

Weirdly enough, that sounded kind of great.

As disconcerting as it was for me to know Noah had a close female friend (close friend period, really) and as conflicted as I felt about Amanda sometimes, I had to admit: she was pretty cool. Not only was she easy to like, but she was the kind of person you wanted to like you *back*.

Noah got up and slid his arm round my waist. His touch was electric. The rest of the world seemed to fade to gray and all that I could think about was his arm on me, even through my T-shirt and jacket.

'Well, we're gonna head out of here,' Noah said. 'Lee, buddy, you desperately need to take a shower. Meet you guys downstairs at six for dinner?'

We'd just about made it to Noah's room before I caved and grabbed him for another kiss.

God, I'd *missed* him.

Chapter 7

Snuggled into Noah's side that night, I wondered if he'd been right. Maybe we *should* just stay inside, right here, and not leave the room at all. Sure, dinner had been nice, and I was excited to see more of Boston . . . but right then, lying with my head on his chest and his arm round me, his fingers playing with the ends of my hair, I didn't ever want to be anywhere else. It was *perfect*.

He nuzzled his nose against my forehead before kissing my cheek. 'I missed you. You should visit more.'

'Maybe *you* should visit more, if you miss me so much.'

'You drive a hard bargain, Evans.'

'You know what else I drive? Three thousand miles just to see you.'

Noah laughed. 'Please. You had a great time driving three thousand miles. Even if you were kind of stinky by the end.'

I gave a cry of indignation and pushed at him. 'Shut up! I was not! I practically *bathed* in deodorant on the way here.' I hoped he didn't see me blushing. I *knew* we should've found somewhere to take a shower before arriving.

'I'm just glad you're here,' he told me, pulling me closer and tilting my chin up to kiss me properly. I curled in tighter to his side and parted my lips as the kiss deepened. I didn't ever want to leave.

'So,' he said, when we finally broke apart, 'are you and Lee really planning to go to Europe next year?'

I scoffed. 'Hardly. You know what he's like. We say a lot of stuff like that. Why? Were you hoping to come meet us at the Dali museum in Barcelona?'

Noah chuckled. 'She likes art, okay? Levi likes cooking French pastries.'

'He's moved on to Italian desserts now,' I said. Levi and his little sister had always baked, but ever since Levi had started watching *The Great British Bake Off* on Netflix he'd really thrown himself into it, exploring new recipes and methods and foods. I wasn't a great cook, but I was more than happy to sit around talking to him while he baked and help him taste-test afterward.

'No, I was just thinking,' Noah said. 'About us. Next year. When you're in college, too. We're gonna have to coordinate more. You know, plan trips home on the same weekend. Maybe meet halfway.'

'I don't even know where I'm going to college yet,' I mumbled, fidgeting with the edge of the bedsheet.

'Sure, but when you get an offer –'

'If,' I corrected him. The whole process of college applications had stressed me out to breaking point. I was excited to go to college, but the idea of graduating high school and maybe growing apart from the Flynn brothers filled me with apprehension. It kind of soured the whole college thing – more than a little.

'*When*. When you get an offer and you pick a college, we'll have to figure something out. I don't think I can go this long without seeing you again. It's been driving me crazy.'

I laughed. I loved it when he said things like that. Sometimes I worried I was too clingy, but then he'd say exactly what I was feeling and I'd stop worrying.

What did I have to worry about?

I hooked my leg over Noah's and kissed him again.

We were *perfect*.

The next night, there was an open-mic comedy night at a coffee shop, complete with low lighting, slightly-too-loud music and beer bottles scattered on tables amid coffee cups and little plates of cake.

'What kind of coffee shop sells beer?' I asked.

'I don't know, but they didn't card me,' Lee said, setting down a beer in front of me, then another for him, one for Noah and a white wine for Amanda. 'I guessed you weren't a beer kind of girl.'

'Only when it's beer pong,' Amanda said, taking her wine and gesturing at Noah with it. 'Me and this guy are unbeatable.'

Lee laughed. 'You're gonna have to teach Elle a thing or two.'

'Me? Please. *You're* awful at it.'

'Only when I'm drunk.'

'Isn't that kind of the point?' Amanda asked, laughing. 'You guys are gonna love tonight, I promise.'

'Remind me how this works, exactly?'

Amanda explained it to me again. People signed up for fifteen-minute slots to do their stand-up comedy set. An MC (who was, she and Noah swore, a semiprofessional comedian and totally hilarious) ran the night, so you were guaranteed at least some laughs.

'But the best part is the heckling,' she told me, with a wicked grin. 'Everyone gets heckled. They know that's basically part of the deal when they sign up. And people really don't hold their punches. Most of the time, the hecklers are funnier than the comedians.'

'Isn't that kind of awful? Don't they find it really humiliating?'

'Oh, no.' She waved a hand. 'They all expect it. Here, if you don't get heckled you're not doing it right.'

'Just don't heckle the MC,' Noah told us.

'He speaks from experience,' Amanda confided, leaning across the table and grinning at us. 'Made that mistake his first time here.'

'Let's not, huh?' Noah gave her a sidelong glance, his mouth stretching into a smirk. I felt a familiar flare of jealousy as they shared a smile over some story I didn't know. I took a sip of my beer, hoping I could swallow down the jealousy, too. I didn't like it – not one bit – especially when I knew how stupid I was being. I was really starting to understand how Rachel felt around me and Lee sometimes.

It wasn't long before the coffee shop had filled up. The lights dimmed and a spotlight shone on to the stage. The latest Taylor Swift song started playing, and a guy in a red bomber jacket ran out on stage. The crowd clapped and I joined in.

The MC had an afro, thick-rimmed glasses, a gap in his teeth and a winning smile. He was maybe in his twenties. His clothes were casual but stylish, and he swung his arms above his head, shouting, 'Come on, you guys! Is that all you've got?'

Noah and Lee whooped from our table, and so did a couple more people.

'Yeah, that's more like it! All right, folks, I'm Jay, I'm your host for the night – for my sins.' The applause and cheers died down and gave way to laughter. 'And, boy, I hope you've all had a few stiff drinks, because we have got one helluva line up for you tonight.'

Jay's bit lasted maybe five minutes. He had all of us eating out of the palm of his hand, everyone wheezing with laughter. He picked on a couple of people from the crowd to taunt, but they all took it in stride.

'We got any newcomers tonight?' he asked. A couple of people stuck their hands up nervously.

I was one of them. Amanda shot to her feet then jabbed a finger at me and grabbed Lee's wrist, hauling his arm into the air.

'Right here we do!'

'Amanda!' I hissed.

Jay climbed off the stage and walked over to us with his microphone. 'Howdy-doo, newbies. What're your names?' He stuck the microphone right in Lee's face.

'I'm Lee. That's Elle.'

'What've we got here? Double date?' He pulled a sympathetic face at Amanda. 'Oh, honey, what happened to the guy with the glasses you were with last time?'

'He's MC-ing tonight,' she shot back.

A chorus of whooping filled the room, and my jaw dropped open as I looked at her.

She'd had all that stuff to tell us about how tonight would be and she forgot to mention possibly *the most important part*?

'Hey, maybe you've at least bagged yourself a funny guy this time,' he said, clapping Lee on the shoulder. 'And what about you, with the space buns? This your hot date for the night?' He gestured at Noah.

'You betcha,' I said.

'And where are you from?'

'California.'

'Ooh, out-of-towners! Slumming it here on the East Coast. In that case, we'd better make sure we give them a good show tonight, huh, everyone?'

He winked at me and did a finger-gun signal at Lee that he somehow pulled off as totally cool and not at all lame, then he bounded back up on to the stage.

'Now, we'll be kicking things off tonight with recently divorced chemistry professor Dave.' There was a chorus of 'awwh' at this, and Jay made a show of taking out his phone and peering over the top of his glasses at it. 'Guess chemistry isn't his strong suit after all, huh? Now, Dave is forty-five, has no kids, is a Sagittarius, five-ten, and – oh, nope, that's his Bumble bio.'

While we were all still laughing, Jay summoned amateur comedian Dave on to the stage to a politely encouraging smattering of applause. Lee caught my eye from his seat next to Amanda. His cheeks were flushed and pink from laughing, a smile splitting across his face. I knew exactly what he was thinking: if this was what college life was going to be like, we were going to *love* it.

My heart sank. I looked back at the stage, barely listening as recent-divorcé and chemistry professor Dave stammered through the start of his set.

If this was what college life was going to be like, yeah, we'd love it . . . but would it be anything like this if we ended up at different colleges? Would Lee be the one making fabulous, flawless new friends like Noah had with Amanda? Would he even need me any more?

Stomach churning, I had the realization, which I hated, that I felt like I'd already lost him. Which was utterly ridiculous. I hated it as much as I hated feeling jealous of Amanda. I took another sip of my beer and tried to focus on the act on stage, but the feeling stuck with me.

Meanwhile, Dave's act only got stronger the more he was heckled. His humor was self-deprecating to the point where most of us were cringing in our seats. One story had us all practically dying from second-hand embarrassment, but somehow it worked. By the time he left the stage, people were cheering.

'What do you guys think?' Amanda asked as Jay returned to introduce the next act (nineteen-year-old Hailey who had just returned from a gap year in Asia).

'This is the *best thing*,' Lee enthused.

'It's great,' I agreed, but I sounded as half-hearted as I felt. I couldn't shake the idea of Lee replacing me with some shiny new friend if we ended up at different colleges.

Noah's arm was draped across the back of my chair and he leaned forward, arm coming up round my shoulders, to murmur, 'Everything okay?'

Ugh, I was being so pathetic. I'd come all the way to Boston to have the best spring break ever with my best friend and my boyfriend and here I was moping over something that probably wouldn't even happen.

I really needed to get hold of myself.

I turned my head to smile at him more sincerely. 'Yeah. Everything's great.'

He smiled back and kissed me briefly before we turned our attention back to the stage. We were just in time to catch Hailey's first punchline, which fell completely flat and opened the floor to the hecklers.

Noah's fingers drifted in light patterns at the back of my neck, sending a shiver down my spine. He leaned forward again to press a kiss just below my ear. Somehow I managed to forget how paranoid I'd been just a few minutes before, and I went back to enjoying the night.

'She's definitely flirting with him,' I said.

Noah scoffed, leaning back in his chair and turning to me. 'She's not.'

'She is! Look! Look at her touching her hair.'

'So, she's into him because she's touching her hair?'

'Well, yes – I mean – not – shut up!' He started laughing at me and I swiped his arm.

It was three acts into the night and there was a break. Amanda had gone to join the too-long line for the restroom and Lee was back at the counter to grab more drinks . . . and a girl was flirting with him. She didn't look much older than us, but she definitely struck me as a 'college girl'. She had tattoos on her wrist and she was wearing a flannel shirt with the sleeves rolled up and a blue beanie over her short choppy hair. Which she kept fiddling with. As I watched, she put a hand on Lee's shoulder and laughed at something he said. He'd turned back to the bar . . . bartender? Barista? Bar-someone, to put in his order. The girl looked visibly disappointed when he didn't offer to get her a drink.

'He's completely clueless,' Noah said, shaking his head. 'Don't ever let him break up with Rachel. He'll never manage to date another girl.'

'Should we go rescue him?'

Noah sighed, but he got up from the table. As he did, a man collided with him and slopped his coffee on to Noah's shoes.

'Hey, watch it,' Noah grumbled.

'Sorry, man. Didn't see you there.'

I held my breath, watching Noah closely. I remembered when guys would knock into him at parties. Their shoulders would barge against each other, they'd square off, push at each other, and someone would throw a punch. Almost every time it would turn into a fight.

I glanced down at Noah's hands, but they didn't curl into fists like I expected. He didn't drop his shoulders or clench his jaw or –

Noah raised his hand, but to pat the man's shoulder. 'It's fine. Don't worry about it.'

The guy walked off. Noah made to go up to the bar to see Lee, but I caught his elbow and tugged him back.

'Hey. What was that?'

'Hmm? Oh, it's no big deal. It's just coffee.' He shook his foot.

'No, I mean . . .' I stood up, tilting my head back to look him in the eye better, unable to keep the frown off my face. I knew Noah had changed since going to college. He'd grown up a *lot*, but . . .

I was so not used to this. 'Any other time, you'd have hit that guy.'

Noah rolled his eyes before looking away from me. 'Oh, come on, Elle. You're exaggerating.'

'Uh, do I need to list every party where Lee or I saw you get into a fight? You punched the garage wall once when you found out your mom accidentally threw away a new part for your motorcycle.'

'I didn't *start* those fights. I've told you. And, yeah, I was mad about the part because it cost, like, a hundred bucks.' He shuffled his feet again. 'It was just some coffee. I'm not about to punch some random dude at comedy night and get arrested for assault.'

I blinked at him.

'Why are you looking at me like that?'

'I just . . .' I blew out a breath, shaking my head and running a hand over my hair. 'You keep surprising me, that's all.'

Now it was Noah's turn to frown. He bit his lip. 'Is that . . . good?'

I laid my hands against his chest. 'It's great. Just . . . different.' I smiled at him. 'Go on. You'd better go help Lee out.'

Still looking a little uncertain, Noah made his way over to Lee. He glanced back at me once.

He'd changed so much since going to college – in all these little ways that kept catching me off guard. He was still cocky and swaggering, and his confidence could almost border on arrogance, but the bad-boy reputation he'd built for himself in high school was long gone.

I'd always known Noah was a good guy. He'd looked out for me and Lee when we were freshmen and he always let us invite our friends to his parties. But every time I'd seen him since he'd gone to college . . .

Well, like I said: he kept surprising me. He just seemed so . . . grown-up.

I knew that was a good thing. He seemed more like himself now. Happier and more easygoing than he used to be. But . . . sometimes it scared me. What if he changed so much that he wasn't my Noah any more? What if he became completely different to the Noah I fell in love with?

I watched him hook Lee into a headlock, ruffling his hair and laughing when Lee elbowed him after scrabbling out of the hold. They gathered up the drinks and made their way back to the table. As they drew closer I could hear Noah laying into Lee, teasing him about being so oblivious to the girl flirting with him at the bar. Lee grumbled and pulled faces.

'Shelly, tell him,' he pleaded with me.

'Sorry, buddy. She was definitely into you.'

Lee pulled a face again, sucking on his teeth and sighing through his nose. He gave me a grave look. 'Never let me screw things up with Rachel. I'll never find another girlfriend ever again.'

Noah and I exchanged a glance and I bit back a grin. Noah winked at me and reached for his drink. I got a warm feeling in the pit of my stomach, and I reassured myself that no matter how much Noah changed at college, he'd always be my Noah.

Chapter 8

The next couple of days blew by in an instant. Noah and Amanda took Lee and me out to breakfast at some hipster place, where the oatmeal came in mason jars and the bacon was high-quality organic stuff that made your mouth water just to smell it. They showed us around campus and took us to a bar they liked that held underage theme nights for college students. We ordered pizza and ate it in Amanda's dorm room over a game of Risk, and we went into the city so Noah and Amanda could show Lee and me their favorite haunts.

Noah and Lee got a little tired of me wanting to stop every couple of yards to take pictures, but Amanda could not have been a more obliging photographer. She climbed halfway up a tree to get a cute shot of me outside a brownstone with the most adorable cherry blossoms and planters, and she wheedled the boys into shining their phone torches at the right angle to get a photo of me hanging off a lamppost like I was in *Singing in the Rain*.

It was a wonderful couple of days, but . . . on a completely selfish level, I was relieved when Lee packed up his car to drive out to Brown to meet Rachel and her parents. And, fine, okay, I *knew* that made me a terrible person, but I had hardly seen Noah all year and, so far, we'd hardly spent any time with just the two of us.

So, despite a completely wonderful couple of days hanging out in a group, I wasn't exactly sorry to be standing beside Lee's Mustang. He shoved a handful of empty candy-bar wrappers at me that we'd missed when we cleared the garbage out from our road trip.

'Text me when you get there safe. And say hi to Rachel from me.'

'Yes, *Mom*.' He rolled his eyes but grinned. 'You take care of yourself too, Shelly. No wild parties, no heavy drinking, all that jazz . . .'

'Yes, *Dad*,' I shot back at him. 'I'll see you in a few days?'

'That you will, kid.'

He pulled me in for a hug and, as we parted, he gave me a sloppy kiss on the cheek and I ruffled his hair.

After I'd waved Lee off, I walked back to the dorms, where Noah was waiting for me. 'You sure you'll be able to cope without him?'

'It's only a couple of days,' I scoffed. But he had a point. Lee and I had hardly *ever* been apart. The few family vacations we'd had in the last few years we often took together. When we were kids, we'd beg our parents to let the other one come along. They gave in when we were eight, and we didn't make it an easy habit for them to quit.

'It'll be good practice for you guys, in case you don't end up at Berkeley together,' Noah said nonchalantly, throwing his arm round my shoulder and drawing me close. His nose nuzzled against mine. 'Never too late to put in an application for a school somewhere near Boston, you know . . .'

Instead of answering him, I said, 'Guess we've got some time to ourselves.' I ran my finger over the motif on his T-shirt.

Noah drew me even closer, until I was flush against him. 'Oh, yeah?'

'There you guys are!'

I couldn't help gritting my teeth. Amanda might have a cute British accent and be infectiously likeable, but right then, I wanted to shove her back through the door, grab Noah's hand, and run.

'Great news. A bunch of us are going to Shay's tonight. We'll grab some dinner there, too. You'll love it, Elle. It's like, sort of a dive bar, but kind of cute? I mean, they have a brie plate. It's to *die* for. And the Riesling is delicious.'

All I could do was stare slack-jawed into the expanse of Noah's chest in front of me. Brie plates? Riesling? I suddenly felt totally out of my depth. And, besides, I just wanted to spend the evening with Noah. Surely *that* didn't make me a bad person, wanting some alone time with my boyfriend?

I looked at Noah, hoping he'd turn it down on behalf of both of us.

But he was smiling at Amanda and saying, 'Awesome. You'll love it, Elle. And you'll get to meet everyone.'

'Am I a terrible person?'

Levi didn't hesitate. 'Absolutely. The worst. I mean, come on, Elle. What kind of monster wants to *spend time* with their significant other instead of carrying on the group hang for, like, day number four? Reddit would definitely agree. You are in the wrong here.'

'Levi, I'm serious.'

Noah was in the shower. I dithered in the hallway, my shoe wedged in the door to keep it open. I'd told Noah, after we'd hung out with Amanda for a little while longer, that it would've been nice to spend some time just us, but he didn't seem to get it. He just kept telling me how much fun it would be and how much I'd love it.

So, I'd done the only thing I could do at that point.

I'd called my good buddy Levi.

After Lee, I'd class Levi as my best friend. And I didn't want to complain to Lee about it because I didn't want him to think I'd resented him being around the last few days. It'd be a kick in the face if he thought I was picking Noah over him. Especially after he'd just driven all the way across the country with me so I could come and see my boyfriend.

Levi, though, he got it. He'd had a serious relationship back in Detroit, before he'd moved to California. He'd been in love. He got this kind of thing more than the other guys did. And sometimes it was good to have someone to talk to that wasn't Lee.

'Did you tell him you didn't want to go hang out with everyone?'

'Yeah, but . . . I didn't push it. That also makes me sound like a jerk. You know, like, "No, Noah, I don't want to hang out with any of your friends. I don't want to go out and do things and be sociable on your spring break."'

'Hmm, okay, that's tough. Can you fake being sick and stay in?'

I kicked at the doorframe, scrunching up my nose. 'No. He'd stay back to look after me and it's pretty obvious I'm not sick.'

'Cramps?'

'For a period he knows I had last week?'

'Man, you guys are close.'

'Lee's mom drilled it into her sons pretty early on that periods are nothing to be embarrassed about. She never wanted me to feel awkward about it. Especially when it's just my dad and brother at home.'

'She's a sweetheart.' Levi was quiet for a minute. 'But, I mean, cramps could still work.'

I rolled my eyes, but he'd made me smile at least. 'I'm just gonna have to tough it out. Maybe it'll just be dinner and we'll head home.'

'Don't bet on it, Elle. You're hanging with cool college kids now.'

'Hey, I called you to make me feel better. You're being the worst friend.'

'I'll send you some memes to make up for it. The plum poem is making the rounds on Twitter.'

'Ugh, again?'

'You know I'm a big fan of poetry memes, Elle.'

He was. He'd sent me, like, fifteen different haikus about a viral meme a couple of weeks ago. It was niche. But it *was* pretty funny.

'I gotta get back to work. My break's almost up.'

'Sure. Thanks, Levi.'

'Any time. Let me know how it goes. Have fun!'

'I'll try,' I mumbled and hung up. I sighed and kicked the doorframe again. I went back into the room. Noah was out of the shower, already dressed and rubbing a towel over his hair.

'Hey, who were you talking to?'

'I was just on the phone.'

'Lee? He there already?'

'No, it was – it was Levi.'

Noah nodded. It was awkward – he was obviously trying to look nonchalant. He shrugged one shoulder, still nodding. 'Cool, cool.'

'Just catching up. He was on his break at work.'

'Cool.'

I appreciated how much Noah was trying. It was how I tried not to be jealous of Amanda.

Except Noah hadn't kissed Amanda. But I *had* kissed Levi.

I stepped up behind Noah, wrapped my arms round his torso and pressed a kiss into his shoulder. I could feel how tense he was. 'I love you.'

He relaxed. 'Love you too, Elle.'

I hesitated. All we were getting was a couple of stolen hours here and there – and most of them when we were tired and going to bed after such a busy day with Amanda and Lee. It *wasn't* selfish of me to want an evening with just the two of us; Levi would have told me straight if he thought so.

'You sure you don't wanna stay in tonight?' I murmured. 'We could start watching that new series on Netflix, the one with the detective . . .'

'Don't tell me you're nervous about meeting my friends, Shelly.' Noah turned round. He put his hand on my cheek and his thumb tilted my chin up to look at him as he smiled crookedly at me, his eyes sparkling. 'Or is it because they're college kids?'

I knew I could have just been honest with him, but, hey, there was always tomorrow. We still had time before Lee returned and we headed back to California. What was one more night sharing Noah with his friends?

I threw my hands in the air and said, 'Okay, you caught me. I'm worried I'll look like a total dork in front of your cool football-playing, Toni Morrison-reading, Riesling-drinking college friends.'

'Trust me, Elle.' His other hand came up to cup my cheek and he bent to kiss me. 'They'll love you.'

Chapter 9

Our one night with Noah's college friends turned into a day at a gallery with them, then another night at Shay's.

Honestly, I didn't hate it. After the initial intimidation (and irritation) wore off, I realized they were really easy to get on with, and a lot of fun. One of Noah's buddies from football was a total movie buff, so we ended up talking a lot about a few I'd seen lately. Amanda's friend she'd stayed with while Lee was here was even clumsier than me and incredibly funny. Apparently, she was a regular at coffee shop comedy nights.

I was scared I wouldn't be able to keep up with what they talked about. I didn't know why I was so scared about it; I had no problem talking to Amanda or Noah. But this felt . . . different somehow. I was relieved to find out that even when they talked about something in the news or to do with politics – or even just a funny viral video – I was part of the conversation. I had something to say. I had an opinion.

It made me *excited* for college in a way I hadn't been yet.

But, admittedly, it was still frustrating to spend so much of my precious time with Noah around other people, too. So, just before Lee was due to come back, I was thrilled when Noah and I suddenly had an entire day to ourselves.

We spent the morning watching a movie.

Well. Okay. Maybe there wasn't exactly a lot of *watching* the movie, and a lot more making out.

June called to check in when we were *actually* watching the movie, so while Noah answered the phone, I dragged myself out from under the comforter to go and take a shower. I shivered once I was out of bed. It was cold – something I was only noticing now I wasn't covered in blankets and snuggled up next to Noah's warm body.

I took some time putting on my makeup and picking out an outfit.

'Don't say you're getting all dressed up for me,' Noah practically purred from the bed, stretching out. 'Why don't you come cuddle?'

'Nope. We're going out.'

'But it's, like, forty degrees out.'

Yeesh.

I steeled myself, pursing my lips and squaring my shoulders as I met Noah's eye, doing my best to look serious. 'Nope. Lee gets back tomorrow evening so this is the only day I really have with *you*.'

I returned to the mirror to finish doing my eyeliner. Shoot. My eyes looked totally different. Ninety per cent of the time, I sucked at eyeliner. I'd been hoping today would fall into the ten per cent where by some miracle, it worked out.

I rooted through my bag for my makeup remover, telling Noah, 'Let's go out.'

He chuckled and threw his arm behind his head. 'Where?'

'Just . . . out. Anywhere. Let's just go hang out.'

'We could walk by the river?'

The hopeless romantic in me couldn't stop the sudden burst of romance-novel-worthy images that sprang to mind. The two of us basking in the golden glow of a sunset, hand in hand and smiling as we walked along a river. In my mind, the Eiffel Tower was also in the background.

Not exactly Massachusetts. But still. It sounded *so* cute.

'That sounds perfect.'

Noah obligingly climbed out of bed, stopping to kiss me before he went to take a shower.

I made two more attempts at my eyeliner. It got worse with each try, so by the time Noah was out of the shower, I'd just removed my third and final try. So much for the elevated even-cooler-girl look I was going for. (Amanda and her friends all wore perfect eyeliner. Maybe I could ask them to share their secrets with me.)

I was sitting on the bed pulling my boots on when Noah placed his hands either side of my hips and leaned over me, his lips finding mine. They were soft and light, but the kiss was firm. His body pressed against mine and I found myself lying back on the comforter.

'Noah . . .' I sighed, but suddenly I wasn't rushing to get out of there and stop making out with him. Noah mumbled something back against my lips that I didn't catch, and I didn't bother asking him to repeat it. The kiss deepened and I trailed my fingers through the back of his hair.

'Hey, watch it,' he said, pulling away and patting his hair back down. 'You're the one who wanted to go out. I just did my hair specially.'

'Please.' I snorted. 'You ran a comb through it.'

'Exactly.'

I couldn't even bring myself to care that my hair was now falling out of its bun where Noah had pressed me down on to the bed. His hands were warm on my skin. As familiar as his touch was, he still drove me completely crazy.

He took my hands in his and stood up, pulling me back into a sitting position.

'Come on. It's meant to rain later.'

I groaned. 'Maybe we should just stay in after all.'

He chuckled. 'Nah, come on. We've got all the rest of tonight to stay in together.'

I huffed, but I finished doing up my boots then grabbed my coat and scarf.

We spent the afternoon walking along the river. It wasn't the Parisian sunset my mind had conjured up – there was a sharp breeze and the sky was gray and heavy with clouds – but it was stunning nonetheless. All those gorgeous old buildings, the river, the trees . . . and actually, the cold weather only seemed to add to the atmosphere. There weren't a lot of people out, but more than I'd expected to see. None of them seemed quite as bundled up against the cold as I was.

We stopped at a cafe for lunch and grabbed sandwiches and drinks – hot chocolate for me and coffee for Noah. We split a muffin and I noticed that Noah gave me the bigger half.

'I can't believe you're leaving the day after tomorrow,' Noah sighed. 'You really can't stay longer?'

'We have to get back. I haven't done, like, *any* schoolwork or studying this whole trip. So I have that to look forward to. And my dad's got a conference upstate, so I have to be on babysitting duty for Brad for two days, remember?'

'Oh, yeah. I mean . . . couldn't he stay with my parents? They wouldn't mind.'

I shook my head. Sure, he could, and the Flynns would be happy to look after him, and Brad wouldn't mind much, but . . .

Well, he was *my* kid brother. After Mom died and whenever Dad was at work, it had always been my responsibility to look after him. It suddenly hit me that if I did go away to college, maybe that wouldn't be my responsibility anymore.

I wasn't sure how I felt about that.

Noah misread my silence and reached out to take my hand. 'Hey. It's okay. I'll be home again before you know it. It'll fly by. Trust me.'

I smiled, turning my hand in his to interlock our fingers. It wasn't exactly the reassurance I wanted, but somehow it helped anyway.

After we left the cafe, Noah wrapped his arm round my waist. 'You've been kind of quiet the last few days, you know. Everything okay?'

I didn't really feel like talking about college and how much everything would change, but . . . Noah looked so concerned. His bright blue eyes focused on mine like they could see right through me and I caved just a little.

'It's just . . . weird, that's all. Seeing you with all your new friends. Seeing you with *friends*, I guess.'

He chuckled. 'You say that like I was a total loner at high school.'

'Close friends,' I corrected. 'You're just – you're all grown-up, all of a sudden. It's, like, every time I see you, I find something new that's changed. At the comedy night I said you keep surprising me, and you do, and that's not – it's not a bad thing, Noah, it's just that . . .' I drew away from him slightly. I looked at my feet as I sucked in a breath. 'I get worried that you'll change and want to be with someone else, and that everything that makes us *us* will be gone.'

I dragged my eyes back to Noah's face, only to see his features crumple. His eyebrows knitted together, his mouth twisted down on one side and his eyes were full of warmth. He reached out, and stroked my cheek with his thumb.

'Elle, I swear, you have nothing to worry about. *Nothing* is going to change the way I feel about you. You broke up with me and I was three thousand miles away and I *still* couldn't get you out of my mind. I love you. Nothing will change that.'

I couldn't help sniffling, and I buried my face in his chest to give myself a second to blink away the threat of tears.

He was such a sweetheart under that tough exterior.

'You look cute like this,' I told him. I drew back and ran my hands over his shoulders. He was wearing a grey beanie and had a blue knitted scarf wrapped round his neck, tucked into his puffy black coat. His hands were buried in his pockets. I had my hands looped round his biceps. His cheeks were flushed pink from the cold, the tip of his nose turning red in the wind, and he'd tucked his chin into his neck in an effort to keep warm.

'Like what?' he asked, twisting his head to look down at me. His breath fogged up in front of his face.

'I've never seen you all bundled up like this. It's very cute.'

'It's cold,' he mumbled. 'Aren't you cold?'

'I'm freaking freezing,' I told him. My toes had gone numb a while ago. These boots were cute, but maybe not winter-proof. I definitely wished I'd worn an extra pair of socks. 'But it's worth it. This is . . .'

I sighed wistfully, looking around. The weather was still bleak. The sky was gray and threatening rain and it was *so darn cold.* It was not exactly the sunny spring break we usually enjoyed back home.

'It's perfect,' I told Noah.

And I meant it.

I'd done a crazy, sort of spontaneous road trip across the country with my best friend. I'd spent the week hanging out with Harvard students. We'd gone to postmodern art installations and cool bars and comedy nights in coffee shops. And now I was standing on the bank of a river basically risking frostbite with Noah's arms wrapped round me and his lips scattering kisses across my cheeks and nose and finally – finally – finding my lips.

It really was the perfect spring break.

Discover a stunning coming-of-age tale by writer and poet Savannah Brown.
Out now.

When her dad dies suddenly, Sydney has questions. The big one: why is June Copeland, the town's golden child, at his funeral?

But as the two teenagers grow closer, Sydney is given a glimpse of a life without the constant darkness.

Until it's clear that the secrets won't go away, and the truth might bring everything crashing down . . .

Read on for an extract!

CHAPTER 1

Seeing the body was supposed to be cathartic, but the man in the lipstick wasn't my dad.

I mean, he was. But he wasn't. There was so little Dad left in him that the emotional experience wasn't too dissimilar from gazing upon a giant steak in a suit: there was discomfort, and a sick sort of a fascination, but mainly a desire for the moment to end. That sounds callous. Maybe it was. Maybe it was a symptom of over-researching; the night before I had spent hours reading about embalming to prepare myself for what this would be like, and now all I could focus on were his glued-together eyelids, his sewn-shut mouth, and his bloated limbs stuffed into clothes tailored well enough to distract everyone from the fact that he looked like a Jim Henson fever dream.

Benjamin Whitaker, the artist formerly known as Dad, had hugged a telephone pole while travelling at approximately sixty miles an hour. Swerve, smash, gone. Well, not really, but 'swerve, smash, unconscious' doesn't have quite the same punch. The lungs were the problem. The lack thereof. They'd popped like a balloon, which isn't *super*-conducive to living; even so, he'd managed to survive long enough to get to the hospital, but not much longer. And when there was no one left to keep alive, they tried to figure out *why*. Town officials. Police officers. Launched an investigation that only led to more uncertainty. The front of the car had practically melted and there was no way to tell if it'd been faulty brakes or steering or whatever, so the best they could come up with was that maybe he had fallen asleep, or been texting, or suicidal, or maybe there was a deer or a person, or maybe he just wasn't paying attention.

And I'm sure, to the outside observer, any of those possibilities might have seemed realistic. But the outside observer didn't know Dad.

I'm exaggerating about how he looked, by the way. He looked fine. Enough to be recognizable, and underneath the pale foundation and pink lip tint, there was still the time-locked stubble and the square jaw and the taffy-pulled limbs. But the sight of his chest was jarring. A mountain range, all slopes and concavities where the newspaper balled up underneath his shirt had deflated. Then something occurred to me.

'Why the hell is he wearing his glasses?'

Mom turned to me, the outside of her cheek puckering as she gnawed on the inside. She was all red: red lips, red blush, reddish hair wound into a bun. Rushing red blood. Practically taunting him. 'Language, please.'

I said the same thing but with *heck*.

She sighed, because she knew what I was implying. 'It's a symbolic thing, Sydney.' I knew it was a symbolic thing.

I just sometimes liked to say stuff I wasn't really thinking. Because I was actually thinking about the corpse of my dad being lowered from the ceiling on a swing, singing a soulful rendition of *Rainbow Connection* with Miss Piggy.

Mom looked me up and down. Just as stoic as I was; she wouldn't cry here either. 'Straighten your skirt, honey. You're all crooked.'

I didn't know where I was crooked, but I believed her – she knew more about skirts than I did – so I did some miscellaneous smoothing until she seemed satisfied. I wasn't sure why she cared. ('Well, yes, the service was lovely, but that girl's lower half was a bit off-centre, don't you think?')

'I'm gonna fix myself up before everyone gets here,' she said. 'Do you want to come?' She wasn't asking me to come so much as she was suggesting I should.

'I don't need to fix myself up.'

Mom was about to protest but seemed to be informed by Dad's ghost that she should drop it, and walked off alone, the ugly carpet dulling the tap of her stilettos to a thud.

Crawford Funeral Home was completely depressing. Because of the light, I think. It was a sickly yellow, leaking on to stiff-looking armchairs and fake potted plants and paintings of places more beautiful than here. The paintings were the only indication that a world existed outside that place; there were windows, but they were the approximate size and shape of a keyhole, and something about the awful baroque pattern on the walls made it seem like they were slowly closing in on you. I wasn't claustrophobic often, but in here, each breath felt itchy and earned. That might've been the intention, though – to make you feel like you were the one about to be buried.

But Rick Crawford seemed right at home. He was the undertaker, well groomed and stout, and spoke with a drawl. The Crawfords had owned the place for generations, and the guy looked like he hadn't been born, but had just crawled out of a vat of formaldehyde. I wondered if he grew into the death or the death grew into him. Anyway, it couldn't have been an easy job. Especially not here, since I was sure he would have recognized at least half the people he had to drag on to the slab every morning. Sort of like Dad. Dad was the only therapist in Pleasant Hills, and I bet that, collectively, he and Rick Crawford knew most of the place's dirty secrets, living and dead.

Our family was small – Dad's parents had died young and Mom wasn't close to hers – so the people who started to trickle in were only faintly familiar. Old family friends. ('Your hair's so long now, wow, strawberry blond, you have your mom's freckles, wow, junior year already? Wow, wow, wow.') Teachers I'd had who felt some sense of obligation to me. Bible-thumpers. Tongue-chewers. The women Mom knew from the gym, from her Tupperware parties, who said things like 'It was his time' over and over again. And there were a lot of strangers – patients. Thanked us for everything Dad had done for them. I knew none of them, which meant Dad had succeeded; he'd always made a point of keeping me away from that part of his life, from the cars pulling up before school and after school and on

Sundays, from the murmurs and more-than-murmurs from behind the office door, from the weights fastened one by one to the heavy, rolling skin underneath his eyes.

But now they were all here, staring me in the face, and any one of them could have done it.

Olivia and I were best friends mostly because we were supposed to be. We had barely anything in common besides the fact that fate had dictated we were to live on the same cul-de-sac, her at three o'clock and me at twelve, but she let me talk about movies and I let her talk about everyone and everything else. She was the high school's chief theatre tech, a social butterfly, had other friends. Me, not so much. Either way, we'd made an unspoken agreement to see out the rest of our formal education careers together; I don't think either of us had anticipated that the agreement would include funeral attendance, but she was here, and although I wouldn't tell her, I was grateful.

'Oh, God,' she said when she noticed I was staring. She looked pretty; her dark hair hung in unnatural curls and her cheekbones shimmered even in the dull light. She had single eyelids, and the glittery purple liner she wore kind of looked like it was part of the anatomy of her eye, swirling upwards and narrowing to a point. The shape reminded me of a robin. Pretty. Not really funeral pretty. 'I knew I shouldn't have come like this. I wanted to get ready first thing this morning so, you know, I could stay as long as you needed, without having to rush back, or anything, but Miles's mom wanted us to be ready for pictures at four. Which is so early, right? That's early. And I tried to say that it was too early, but they already made the dinner reservations, and I realize that seems not important compared to –'

'Hey.' I envisioned us standing there until we began to decompose, Olivia still talking while chunks of flesh fell from her skull. I patted her on the cheek. 'Don't worry about it. Deep breaths.'

Olivia squished her mouth into an O and sucked, backwards whistle, and it looked stupid as hell, so I laughed, but someone I didn't know shot me a glance and I folded in on myself. Lowered my voice. 'I don't want to meet and greet any more.' Mom was talking to someone, which meant I could make my escape. 'Let's go hide.'

We managed to sneak away to an inconspicuous hallway near the entrance. I slumped against the wallpaper as Olivia wrung her wrist in her other hand, searching for something to say – unusual for her. 'Do you want to, like, talk?' she asked. 'I read that it's good to talk. You're supposed to express yourself because if you don't, you'll end up spontaneously combusting. Not really, but, you know. Metaphorically. With emotions.'

'I appreciate the fact that you did research, but, no. Not right now.' I shut my eyes, rested the back of my head against the wall, wished to be anywhere else. 'Regular programming. Just . . . talk.'

'All right. Oh! We missed you last night.'

It took me a second to remember: the game. Right. It was the homecoming game, and a Very Big Deal, and she'd invited me along, but to be completely honest, school spirit was at the very bottom of my priorities list, besides eating food and behaving like a normal human being. 'How was it?' I asked, even though I wasn't particularly interested. Anything to keep her talking.

'Yeah, good. We won, obviously. Hooray, go Panthers, go football, so on, so forth. But honestly, it was probably for the best you didn't go, because it was freezing, firstly, and it went on forever. Like, overtime. I thought I was gonna have to get some toes amputated. Oh, and they did the homecoming court stuff. Heath Alderman and June Copeland won king and queen, obviously.' Olivia had a tendency to insist upon the obviousness of non-obvious things, but she wasn't exaggerating this time; Heath Alderman and June Copeland might have actually been bred to be homecoming royalty, like some sort of champion line of miniature schnauzers. 'I have no idea how June did it,' Olivia continued, 'but she was standing out in the field in this beautiful dress which had no sleeves. Zero sleeve. The wind chill was, like, minus three, but she didn't even have a single freaking goosebump. Oh, so, speaking of homecoming things, are you sure you're OK with me going tonight? For real. I don't have to. Miles will get over it. We can just stay in –' she nudged me with her elbow – 'watch a movie or something. Even one of your weird ones.'

Honestly, I didn't want her to go. It was nice to have access to *sound*, some sort of stimulation, but I would have felt guilty asking her to stay. 'Don't worry,' I said. 'Bring me back, uh, a fish cupcake, or something. That's the theme, right?'

‘Oh, all right, let me tell you about the *theme*.’ Apparently, it was a whole thing that student council was split between Roaring Twenties (event coordinator extraordinaire Olivia’s idea) and Under the Sea (not Olivia’s idea; also, apparently, a horrible idea), and they ended up going with Under the Sea, and Olivia went on an admittedly well-constructed tirade about how democracy doesn’t work because most people are too stupid to pick the right answer. Fine. Maybe we did have something in common.

Eventually, Rick called out from the main room that the ceremony was starting. Olivia went back to her parents plural and I sat with Mom in the front row, which was reserved for us. Phew. I was worried we’d be stuck in the cheap seats. I said this to Mom, who told me under her breath to stop it.

‘Er, hello, everyone, thank you for coming,’ Rick began, standing at the podium, clearing his throat in between words. The casket was closed now, so I had to find something else to think about: the way the saliva in Rick’s mouth went stringy as he talked would do. ‘My name is Rick Crawford, I’m a civil celebrant, and it’s truly a privilege to welcome you all to this celebration of Benjamin Whitaker’s forty-six years of life. He was, er, first and foremost, a husband to Rebecca and a father to Sydney.’ He gestured to Mom and me. I felt like I should wave. ‘But he was also a hero to many in our community, and it is with great sadness that we see him off here today.’ He was a nice-enough guy, but as he went on for a bit about the fragility of life and the human experience, it was obvious every other poor wretch had been given the same non-specific speech. It was canned. An ad lib. Insert cause of death, familial relations and religious affiliations here.

And then it was me at the microphone. Felt like I'd just been plucked out of the ether, like this was someone else's funeral I'd accidentally stumbled into, but they were looking at me all dumb and brow-furrowed so I had to say something. 'My –'

The microphone wailed. I stepped back while the collective face of the audience curled into a wince. Apologized. 'Uh, Dad is – well, was. Was.' They stared. Mom ground her teeth. I apologized again. This was awful. 'Um, so . . . Dad really cared about people. About everyone, really. His whole job was listening and empathizing, and that's, you know. That's something.'

Mercifully, a few heads nodded, as if I had said something very important. I knew I hadn't. I had nothing to say. But that wasn't true. I did – just not to these people. If it'd just been me talking into a void, oh, I would've had all kinds of things to say. I would have told the void the one where I'm six, and Dad and I are hiking at the River Styx, the place where I learned to love the world just as much as he did, and we're on the secluded path that runs parallel to the stream, and I go to explore by the swampy pools along the riverbank – looking for tadpoles, or something – and my feet have already disappeared up to my ankles by the time I realize I'm sinking. But Dad hauls me out by my arms, the mud sucking and popping beneath me like I'm a loose tooth. We wash our feet in the stream, watch the mud get swept away with the current, and Dad says he didn't think that anyone has ever been so calm in quicksand. I could have told the one where I'm eight and he lets me watch episodes of *The Twilight Zone* with him after Mom goes to sleep; where I'm eleven and we ride the bumper cars at the county carnival over and over even though he has a bad back; where I'm fourteen and he holds me after the girl breaks my heart; where I'm seventeen and he's sitting in a box to my right and everyone is expecting something of me, and I can't stand it, I really can't, because he shouldn't be dead.

He shouldn't be dead.

I fiddled with the microphone stand, my fingers slipping. 'But why doesn't anybody know what happened? The . . . the car people. The coroner. Whatever. This sort of thing can't just happen.'

At this point, the audience were still on my side – besides Mom, whose spine had got noticeably straighter. They were waiting for me to throw in the twist, the *but*, to share some glorious epiphany about how that was just the way the world is, that sometimes we don't have all the answers, that life is unfair.

'Dad did care about people. But, I don't know. Maybe people didn't extend that same care to him.'

Mom mouthed my name.

'He was told people's most personal stuff on a daily basis. Secrets upon secrets. Dark stuff. And maybe . . .'

At first, I thought maybe I'd been in a highly suggestive state and was experiencing grief-induced hallucinations, because I could have sworn that, near the back of the room, was the homecoming queen.

June Copeland stood with the posture of someone trying not to be noticed, but hunched shoulders don't hide much when you stand six feet in heels and look like her. She had these curls that cascaded down her back and round her shoulders, a foamy waterfall of ringlets so dark that the darkness seemed to fold in on itself like a black hole. In some places, the spirals were uniform, but round the top they burst forth like a halo, cumulus, cotton candy.

Sorry. Got carried away.

She met my gaze and gave me the saddest little smile I'd ever seen. Her cheeks rose as she did; they were a warm brown, the colour of clay, like every terracotta pot in the world had got together and discussed all the reds and the browns until they arrived at the most harmonious combination, then bathed her in the result. But the smile disappeared just as quickly as it had arrived, and I didn't know what to do besides stare.

Mom's hand on my bicep drew me away. 'Come on, sweetie.' I wasn't sure how long I'd been standing there. Maybe a second. Maybe an eternity. I let her drag me off the platform, watched my feet as I stepped down, but when I looked back towards the entrance there was only the black hem of June's dress swaying through the closing door.

I sat. Folded my hands. Collected myself.

As the moment dissolved I became increasingly aware of the eyes aimed at the back of my skull, like worms boring through the marrow. I didn't dare turn to meet them. I felt ridiculous. Thoroughly embarrassed. What had I just done? What had I even been trying to say? If I had been watching myself from where June was standing, I decided, I would have thought I was insane.

Clearly everyone else agreed, because they took Dad to the cemetery without any requests for further autopsies or an impromptu search for clues. They had the decency to wait for me, at least; I opted to travel via bike instead of car behind the procession. And while they lowered him down with the awful creaking straps, I imagined him waking up inside the coffin, clawing at the polished mahogany until his fingernails wore away, and I wanted desperately for them to open it, just to check, just to see. The website had said Pleasant Hills Cemetery was eighteen rolling acres and I had no idea where these walls were coming from, closing in, crushing, *crushing*, and I sucked air into my throat like it might be for the last time.

But that was it. They dropped him in, and that was it.

We lingered for a while longer. Olivia was noticeably gentler with me as she said goodbye, and Mom talked to people who thought I couldn't hear them. Hushed: Sydney seems like she's taking it badly. Oblivious: I think Sydney should see a therapist. Of course. There would be books in Dad's office that accused me of *projection*, of being so averse to the reality of the situation that I had made up some fanciful hypotheses about all the things that could have happened that didn't include the word 'accident'.

And when I pedalled away behind Mom, her trunk full of bouquets that would wilt and food we wouldn't eat, I swore I saw June Copeland at the curve where the hill met the horizon, her black dress playing between the stones.

*

That night, I rolled the funeral over in my head once, twice, again.

Dad laid out on the slab. Dad underground.

It all felt so strange. If someone had told me it hadn't actually happened, I probably would have believed them; when I tried to summon up the memory of it, it felt flimsy, like I couldn't actually hold on to it, like my brain knew it was something too deleterious to keep.

But June Copeland. She was there.

What the *hell* had she been doing? National Honor Society president. The likely salutatorian to Heath's likely valedictorian. I had never even spoken to her. Just admired from afar. Which makes me sound creepy, but we all did it. We were almost expected to. They were paraded around as Pleasant Hills' golden children, as some sort of goal for us, the common folk, to aspire to. Made even more impressive by the fact that June had only moved to Pleasant Hills freshman year from somewhere in California; originally an outsider, she'd assimilated so successfully that she hadn't just become an insider, but now ruled over them herself. Actually, Heath *was* the school president – maybe June was there as some sort of fucked-up first-lady responsibility? But why had she ... looked at me like that? Half like I was pathetic, half like I was pitied, as if I'd been an ant she'd accidentally stepped on but at least respected enough to flick off her shoe.

But maybe it was more than that. The strangers, quiet, with their heads down – maybe it was a thank-you.

Most importantly, though: why did I care?

That's when I got the text.

Them: Hi Sydney.

My nerves stood to attention. There was no name. There wasn't even a number; it was only listed as 'restricted'. And it was nearly three in the morning. Who that I didn't know was texting me at three in the morning?

I typed back with heavy fingers.

Me: Uh hello

Me: Sorry

Me: Who is this?

The ellipses that meant the person was typing appeared below my texts almost instantly. Like the sender had been sitting there. Waiting for my response.

Them: You really think someone killed him?

It was an odd sensation. I still hadn't processed what exactly was going on – generally, too, but in that exact moment – and it was as though my blood wanted to run cold but wasn't sure of it, and had instead opted for lukewarm.

You really think someone killed him?

I didn't know what to say. Wasn't even sure if I should say anything.

So I didn't. Turned my phone off, rolled over in bed, willed myself to sleep until the light outside turned pink.

SPONSORED BY
NATIONAL BOOK tokens

READING IS POWER

- What's the **GREATEST BOOK** you've ever read, the most **POWERFUL STORY** ever told?
- Which **AUTHOR** speaks to you the loudest, who is the **CHARACTER** that **STUCK IN YOUR HEAD** long after you put the book down?
- Which **ILLUSTRATORS** enchant you and make you want to pick up a pen yourself?
- How do you get your **BOOKISH** fix? Downloaded to your phone or do you prefer the feel of a book in your hands?

How do *you* share stories?

Here at World Book Day, **we celebrate books in all their glory and guises**, we love to **think and talk about books**. Did you know we are a **charity**, here to bring books, your favourite **authors and illustrators** and much more to readers like you?

We believe **BOOKS AND READING ARE A GIFT,** and this book is our gift to **YOU.**

#ShareAStory today, in celebration of all the books you love